Why am I....?

a yelodoggie book

by **Ari Wulff**

with Robert McCarty

FREEDOM *Chaser*
B O O K S

Published by FreedomChaser Books
& Who Chains You Publishing
P.O. Box 581
Amissville, VA 20106
FreedomChaserBooks.com

Written and illustrated by Ari Wulff, thewoof.wordpress.com
with Bob McCarty, planetofthedogs.net

Paperback ISBN: 978-1-954039-14-8

Printed in the United States of America

First Edition

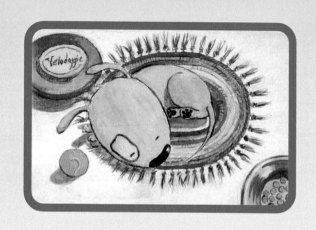

DEDICATION

For "Cakes"

Floyd is a happy dog . . .

With many friends.
Some of them are dogs . . .

Some of them are cats.

Some of them live in the water . . .

Some of them live in the sky.

One day, someone asked Floyd
why he was yellow.

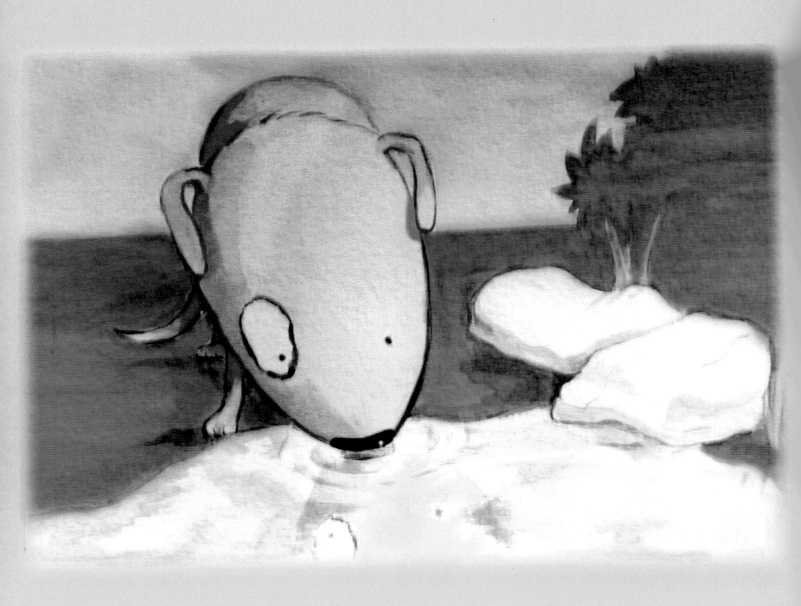

Floyd had never thought about it.
He did not know the answer.

He wasn't a lemon. He wasn't a banana.
He was a dog. "Why **am** I yellow?" he wondered.

Floyd thought a fortune cookie might tell him . . .
but it only said his lucky number was 8.

So Floyd went on a journey to find the answer.

Floyd went to a ranch and
asked the cattle, "Why am I...?"
"Why do we have hooves?" the cattle said.

Floyd went to a farm and
asked a chicken, "Why am I...?"
"Why do I have feathers?" said the chicken.

Floyd went to the zoo and
asked the tortoises, "Why am I..?"
"Why do we carry our homes on our backs?"
said the tortoises.

Floyd asked the rhinoceros, "Why am I...?"
"Why do I have this big horn on my face?"
said the rhino.

Floyd asked the elephant, "Why am I...?"
"Why do I have such a long nose?"
said the elephant.

Floyd asked a crab on the beach, "Why am I...?"
"Why do I have these big pincers?" said the crab.

Floyd asked a fish in the sea, "Why am I...?"
"Why do I live underwater?" said the fish.

Floyd asked some skunks, "Why am I...?"
"Why do we smell funny?" said the skunks.

Floyd even looked for an answer on the moon,
but could not find one.

So Floyd went back home . . .

He tried to find the answer in a crystal ball.

But the answer was nowhere to be found,
and not having an answer bothered him.

So Floyd slept on it . . .

The next day, he spent a long time
in his garden thinking . . .

" I know dogs who are every color of the rainbow," Floyd thought.

"**E**verybody is different.
That's what makes them who they are.
There is nothing wrong with being yellow . . ."

"Because yellow is the color of light and joy, and in their heart of hearts, that's what every dog is made of."

So Floyd went out to play . . .
a happy dog again.

Love the book? Please consider giving *Why Am I?* a review on Amazon and other venues. Your reviews mean the world to our authors.

Thank you!

About the Author and Illustrator

Ari Wulff is an author, artist, and animal advocate.

Wulff is the author of four books: ***Born Without a Tail, Circling the Waggins, How to Change the World in 30 Seconds,*** and ***Parade of Misfits.***

They are also the coauthor of ***Finding Fido***, and the illustrator for the children's books ***Raffy Calfy's Rescue, Smidgey Pidgey's Predicament,*** and ***Squirmy Hermie's Heroics.***

Wulff is the creator of the Yelodoggie character. Find Ari online at **thewoof.wordpress.com**.

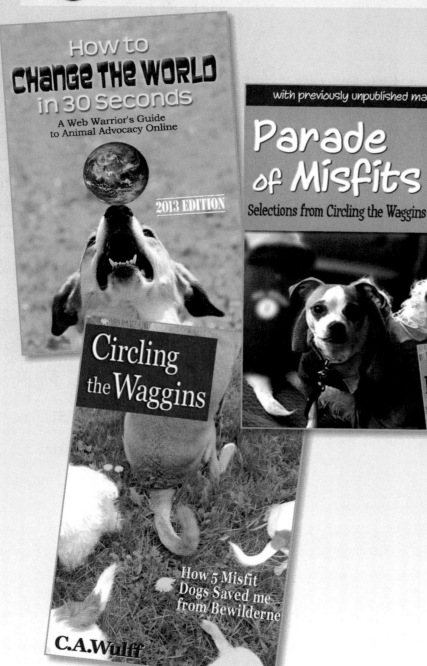

About the Coauthor

Robert McCarty is the author of the ***Planet Of The Dogs*** series of children's books: ***Planet Of The Dogs, Castle In The Mist,*** and ***Snow Valley Heroes, A Christmas Tale.***

He is the founder of Barking Planet Productions and writes the Barking Planet Children's Books blog at **planetofthedogs.net**.

Smidgey-Pidgey's
Predicament

Animal Protector
SERIES

Illustrated by
C.A. Wulff

Animal Protector
SERIES

Squirmy Hermie's
Heroics

Illustrated by
C.A. Wulff

tamira thayne

Animal Protector
SERIES

Raffy Calfy's
Rescue

Illustrated by
C.A. Wulff

tamira thayne

About FreedomChaser Books

At FreedomChaser, we publish books for those who believe people—and animals—deserve to be free

FreedomChaser brings you books that educate, entertain, and share gripping plights of the animals we serve and those who rescue and stand in their stead.

We offer all kinds of stories about all kinds of animals: dogs, cats, rats, cows, pigeons, horses, pigs, snails, bears, and so many more! *Visit our site and read more about us at www.freedomchaserbooks.com.*

Other books from FreedomChaser

FreedomChaserBooks.com

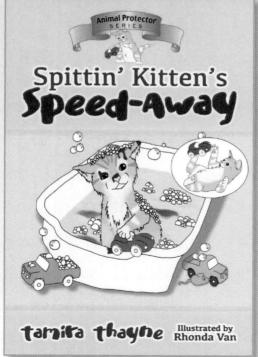